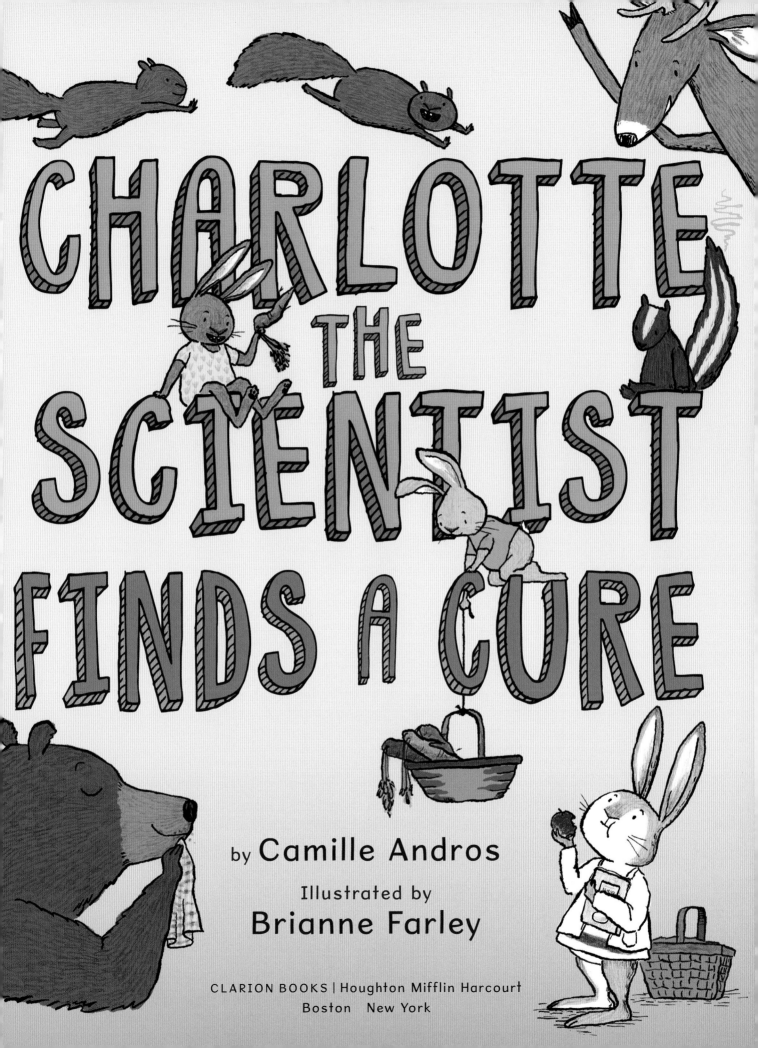

CHARLOTTE THE SCIENTIST FINDS A CURE

by **Camille Andros**

Illustrated by
Brianne Farley

CLARION BOOKS | Houghton Mifflin Harcourt
Boston   New York

Charlotte was a serious scientist.
She spent her days doing research, performing experiments, and solving problems.

Charlotte lived in the forest with her bunny-size family, which was bigger and better than ever.

Because Grandpa had moved in.

Grandpa was wise.

He had many awards.

And when he spoke,
everyone paid attention.

Every day Grandpa visited Charlotte in her lab.

He watched her doing research, performing experiments, and solving problems.

Every day Grandpa said, "Charlotte, you are going to make a real difference in the world."

Charlotte paid attention.

One day Grandpa didn't come to the lab.

He was sick.

And Grandpa wasn't the only one.

A mysterious malady had infected the animals of the forest.

Charlotte wanted to help.

Maybe this was her chance to make a difference.

She swapped her magnifying glass for a stethoscope, her protective glasses for a mask and gloves, and got to work.

It was time for some serious medical science.

Charlotte would find a cure!

gloves

mask

stethoscope

First, she collected a complete
medical history on each patient.

what seems
to be the
problem?

Next she gave a thorough physical exam.

Patient privacy was
a top priority.

Then she gathered specimens.

Next!

But her results were
inconclusive.

Charlotte was stumped.

The infection was spreading fast, so she imposed a quarantine.

But keeping bunnies in one place was next to impossible.

The birds kept flying away, and skunks stinking simultaneously was proving problematic.

Meanwhile, a team of doctors arrived to visit Grandpa.
Charlotte was eager to share her research and
work with them to find a cure.
But instead, they ignored her.

Charlotte wondered if they were right.

She *was* little.

And the doctors were very smart.

Maybe she should leave it to the experts.

But then she remembered what Grandpa had told her.

She would find the cure herself.

Charlotte dissected the data,

studied the samples,

and plotted out patterns.

Soon, a curious carrot connection emerged.

Everyone who was sick had been eating carrots! In fact, the carrots hadn't looked right for quite some time.

Charlotte formed a hypothesis.

If everyone who was sick had been eating carrots,
then the carrots were what was making everyone sick.

Charlotte consulted the *Comprehensive Compendium of Carrot Conditions.*

It could only be one thing—Funky Forest Fungi.

After careful consideration, Charlotte came up with a second hypothesis.

If eating the infected carrots was making everyone sick, then stopping contaminated carrot consumption could be the cure!

Funky
Forest
Fungi

Charlotte went back to work.

The carrots needed to be cured,

so she created a customized carrot corrective.

Charlotte thought a few sprays a day should do the trick.

It worked!

But Charlotte didn't stop there.
She conducted a clinical trial to see if
eating cured carrots could mend the malady.

It did!

Charlotte realized she didn't need to be the oldest or smartest.

She had stopped the sickness, cured the carrots, and saved the forest!

Charlotte had made a difference.

And best of all was the difference in
how she saw herself.

IN THE LAB WITH
CHARLOTTE

In *Charlotte the Scientist Finds a Cure,* Charlotte uses science to find the cure for the mysterious malady that has infected the forest. Doctors, researchers, and other medical professionals use science to diagnose, treat, prevent, and cure diseases. Many scientific and medical terms are used in the book. You can find their definitions in the glossary.

To learn more about Charlotte and science, be sure to read *Charlotte the Scientist Is Squished*!

GLOSSARY

CLINICAL TRIAL: an experiment that tests the effects of a treatment on a group of individuals

Charlotte conducted a clinical trial to see if eating cured carrots could mend the mysterious malady.

COMPENDIUM: a book about a particular subject

Charlotte consulted the *Comprehensive Compendium of Carrot Conditions* to figure out what was wrong with the carrots.

CONSUMPTION: the act of eating or drinking something

Charlotte thought stopping contaminated carrot consumption could be the cure.

CONTAMINATE: to make harmful, dirty, or impure

The carrots were contaminated by the Funky Forest Fungi.

CORRECTIVE: something that makes a problem better

Charlotte created a customized carrot corrective to treat the contaminated carrots.

DISSECT: to take apart, cut up, or divide in order to study

Charlotte dissected the data in search of the cure.

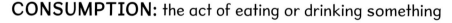
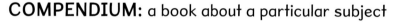

HYPOTHESIS: a best-guess answer to a question; an idea or theory that hasn't been proven yet; usually includes the words "if" and "then"

Charlotte made a hypothesis about the carrots: If everyone who was sick had been eating carrots, then the carrots were what was making everyone sick.

MALADY: a sickness or disease

A mysterious malady had infected the animals of the forest.

MEDICAL SCIENCE: science that involves the prevention and treatment of disease

Charlotte used medical science to find a cure.

QUARANTINE: an order to keep sick people or animals away from those who are healthy

To keep the infection from spreading, Charlotte imposed a quarantine.

SPECIMEN: a sample of a substance used for medical testing

Charlotte gathered specimens from the sick animals.

"I realized I didn't need to be the oldest or the smartest to make a difference. I am good enough just by being myself. Write and tell me how YOU are making a difference either by using science or just by being yourself—at home, with your friends, or in your classroom."

CHARLOTTE THE SCIENTIST
c/o CLARION BOOKS/HMH
3 Park Avenue, 19th Floor, New York, NY 10016

Or email me!
charlotte@charlottethescientist.com

For my Grandpa.
You made a real difference in the world.
I love you and miss you. —C.A.

For Paul and Lori. Thank you, always. —B.F.

Clarion Books • 3 Park Avenue, New York, New York 10016 • Text copyright © 2019 by Camille Andros • Illustrations copyright © 2019 by Brianne Farley All rights reserved. For information about permission to reproduce selections from this book, write to trade.permissions@hmhco.com or to Permissions, Houghton Mifflin Harcourt Publishing Company, 3 Park Avenue, 19th Floor, New York, New York 10016. • Clarion Books is an imprint of Houghton Mifflin Harcourt Publishing Company. • hmhco.com • The illustrations in this book were executed in charcoal, pencil, and ink on paper and colored digitally. • The text was set in Sweater School. • Design by Sharismar Rodriguez • Library of Congress Cataloging-in-Publication Data Names: Andros, Camille, author. | Farley, Brianne, illustrator. • Title: Charlotte the scientist finds a cure / written by Camille Andros ; illustrated by Brianne Farley. • Description: Boston ; New York : Clarion Books, Houghton Mifflin Harcourt, [2019] • Summary: "Charlotte, a budding bunny scientist, ignores the doubters and confidently finds a cure to the mysterious malady affecting the forest"— Provided by publisher. • Identifiers: LCCN 2018035166 | ISBN 9780544813762 (hardback) • Subjects: | CYAC: Sick—Fiction. | Science—Methodology—Fiction. | Science—Experiments—Fiction. | Self-confidence—Fiction. | Rabbits—Fiction. | BISAC: JUVENILE FICTION / Animals / Rabbits. | JUVENILE FICTION / Science & Technology. | JUVENILE FICTION / Social Issues / Self-Esteem & Self-Reliance. | JUVENILE FICTION / Humorous Stories. | JUVENILE FICTION / Family / Multigenerational. Classification: LCC PZ7.1.A565 Cd 2019 | DDC [E]—dc23 LC record available at https://lccn.loc.gov/2018035166 Manufactured in China • SCP 10 9 8 7 6 5 4 3 2 1 • 4500745212